THE STEADFAST
TIN SOLDIER

By HANS CHRISTIAN ANDERSEN

Illustrated by
DAVID JORGENSEN

ALFRED A. KNOPF PUBLISHERS • NEW YORK

This is a Borzoi Book published by Alfred A. Knopf, Inc.

Copyright © 1986 by Random House, Inc., and Rabbit Ears Productions

MANUFACTURED IN THE UNITED STATES OF AMERICA

Designed by Antler & Baldwin Design Group

2   4   6   8   10   9   7   5   3   1

As adapted by Joel Tuber for the video version of
THE STEADFAST TIN SOLDIER
narrated by Jeremy Irons
directed by Mark Sottnick

Library of Congress Cataloging-in-Publication Data
Andersen, H. C. (Hans Christian), 1805–1875.
The steadfast tin soldier.
Translation of: Den standhaftige tinsoldat.
Summary: The perilous adventures of a toy soldier who
loves a paper dancing girl culminate in tragedy
for both of them.
[1. Fairy tales. 2. Toys—Fiction] I. Jorgensen, David, ill. II. Title.
PZ8.A542St 1986 [Fic] 86-2787
ISBN 0-394-88402-7 ISBN 0-394-88299-7 (book/cassette)

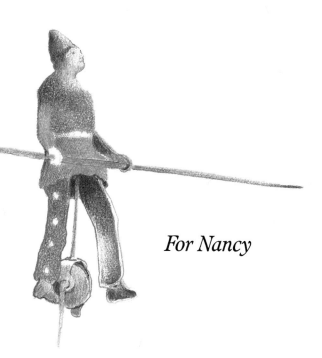

For Nancy

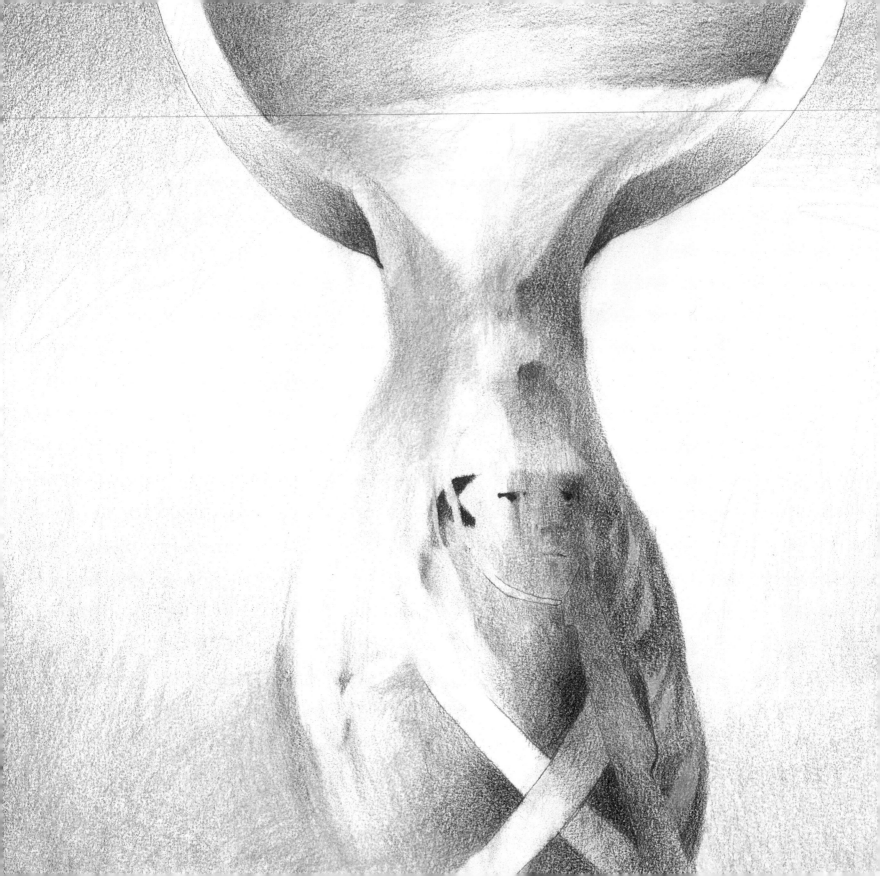

Once there were five and twenty soldiers. They were brothers, for they'd all been cast from the same old tin spoon. It had once been a very beautiful serving spoon with forget-me-nots and tiny hearts entwined around its handle. But then it had fallen into a tinsmith's hands. He had melted it down and cast it into the twenty-five tin soldiers who stood at attention, staring straight ahead.

Each one wore a smart red and blue uniform. And each held a rifle with a tiny bayonet.

But one of the soldiers was different from the rest. He had been the very last to be cast, and there had not been enough metal to finish him, so he was missing a leg. But he was as firm and steadfast on his one leg as the other soldiers were on two. And *he* is the hero of our story.

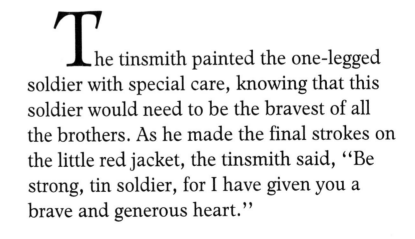

The tinsmith painted the one-legged soldier with special care, knowing that this soldier would need to be the bravest of all the brothers. As he made the final strokes on the little red jacket, the tinsmith said, "Be strong, tin soldier, for I have given you a brave and generous heart."

Then he placed the soldiers in a long wooden box and set them in his shop window.

For days the tin soldiers lay silent in their box, wondering what might become of them. Then, one fine morning, the lid was snapped shut, and the soldiers were jostled as the box was wrapped and carried outside into the cold air.

From inside their wooden box the soldiers could hear excited voices. Then the wrapping was torn away, and the lid flew up.

"Tin soldiers!" shouted a little boy, clapping his hands because he had received them as a birthday present.

Eagerly the boy lifted out the soldiers and stood them, one by one, in neat rows across the polished table top.

The one-legged soldier stood as straight and steadfast as his brothers.

There were many other toys on the table—a slate pencil, a nutcracker, a jack-in-the-box. . . . But the toy that really caught the eye was a cardboard castle. It had turrets and real windows that you could look through, even a tiny drawbridge. It stood at the top of a papier-mâché hill covered with little green trees. In front of the castle was a mirror that looked just like a lake, with white swans swimming about on its silvery surface.

But the most wonderful of all was the person who lived in the castle. She was a tiny paper doll, dressed in pale blue chiffon like a ballerina. Her hair was the color of gold, and over her shoulders she wore a ribbon, held in place by a large metal spangle which shimmered and glowed. "Like a real diamond," thought the tin soldier.

The paper doll's arms were stretched out, as though she were about to embrace someone, and she stood delicately balanced on one leg. She held the other leg behind her in a graceful curve. From his place on the table the tin soldier couldn't see it, and he thought that she, too, had only one leg. His heart went out to her. "How I would like to meet her," he said to himself.

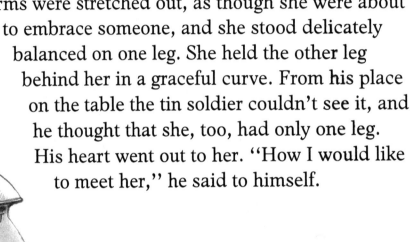

He even dared to think that someday, perhaps, the little ballerina could become his wife. "But she is a princess in a beautiful castle on a hill. And I am just a soldier in a wooden box that I must share with twenty-four others. That would never do for her. Still, I would love to meet her." And the soldier lay down full-length behind the jack-in-the-box where he could watch the lovely dancer.

That evening, at bedtime, a young maid came into the room. She put the soldiers back in their box, but she didn't see the one-legged soldier, so he was left behind. He watched as the maid picked up the ballerina, turned her slowly round and round, and then the maid put her back in the castle.

The house was quiet. Everyone was asleep. Now the toys began to play. They played house and hide-and-seek; they danced and sang.

The four and twenty tin soldiers rattled their bayonets inside their box. They wanted to play, too, but the lid wouldn't budge. The nutcracker turned somersaults. The slate pencil wrote on the blackboard.

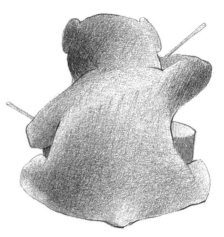

They all made so much noise that the canary woke up and told them what she thought of them. The only ones who didn't move were the tin soldier and the ballerina. She stood at her castle window, and the soldier lay on the table looking up at her. His eyes never left her—not even for a moment.

Then the clock struck twelve. Pop! With a frightening bang, the jack-in-the-box opened. Out sprang a troll with eyes like fire. "Tin soldier! Why aren't you in the box with your brothers?" he screamed. "And why can't you keep your eyes to yourself!"

The tin soldier didn't know what to say, so he remained silent, as if he hadn't even heard the troll. This, of course, only made the troll angrier. "You just wait until tomorrow," he hissed, and then he disappeared into his box.

"What did he mean by that?" wondered the tin soldier.

The next morning the boy came into the room and saw the tin soldier lying next to the jack-in-the-box. He picked him up and placed him on the window sill. It is hard to say exactly what happened next. Maybe it was the wind. Or perhaps the troll had something to do with it. But suddenly the curtain grabbed at the tin soldier, knocking him off balance. He tottered back and forth on the edge of the window sill.

Then, all at once, the tin soldier felt himself falling. Down, down, down he fell, three whole stories, all the way to the street, where his bayonet stuck in the earth between the cobblestones. For what seemed like a very long time the little tin soldier lay there hoping he would be found. Then he heard voices. The boy had fetched the maid to come outside with him to look for the missing soldier. Though they nearly stepped on him several times, they didn't see him.

If only the tin soldier had shouted, "Here I am, stuck between the cobblestones!" But he remained silent because he felt that it was wrong for a soldier to shout when in uniform. The boy and the maid searched for a long time. Then they went back inside.

The tin soldier was left alone. He watched the sun cross the sky and disappear behind the house. Night came, and then the rain—one drop, then another, until it was pouring.

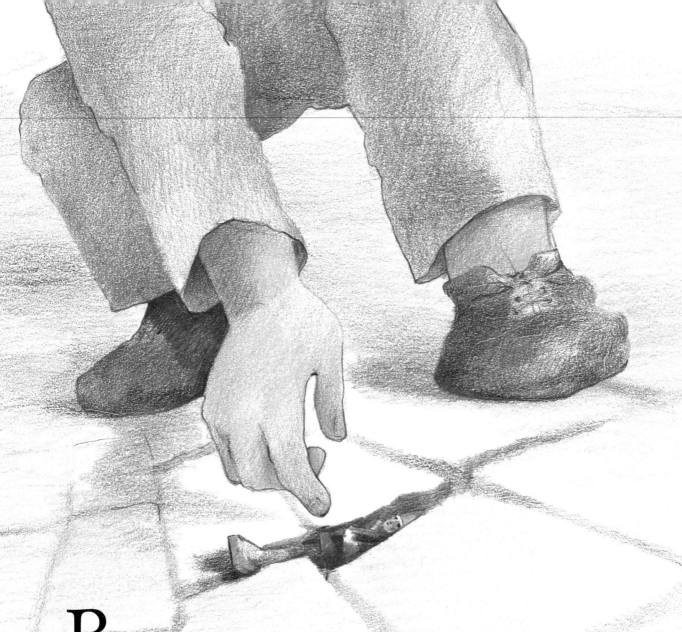

By morning the rain had stopped and the sun shone down on the little tin soldier, still wedged between the cobblestones. Two boys on their way to school walked by. "Look, a tin soldier!"

"He probably isn't much of a soldier. He's only got one leg."

The tin soldier knew he was as good a soldier as any. He wanted to answer the boys, but he said nothing because he didn't want to boast.

"I bet he'd make a good sailor," said the first boy, folding a little boat out of one of his school papers. He put the tin soldier aboard and set him to sail in the gutter. Away went the boat, spinning and bouncing in the rushing stream of rain water. The two boys ran along on the sidewalk, laughing and shouting.

As the boat dipped and turned in the waves, the tin soldier trembled inside himself with fear. But he stood, steadfast as ever, looking straight ahead. "Could this be what the troll meant?"

The boat was approaching the drain that led to the sewer. The two boys saw what was going to happen and tried to grab hold of it. They were too late. The paper boat and the tin soldier fell through the drain, into the darkness.

It was cold in the sewer, and the sound of the rushing water was very loud and frightening. The tin soldier wished he were back with his brothers in the wooden box, and he thought of the ballerina. "If only I could see her again, I wouldn't be so afraid. If only she were here, I wouldn't care if it were twice as dark or cold."

Suddenly a fat gray water rat appeared beside the boat and shouted at the soldier, "Have you got a passport? Show me your passport."

The tin soldier didn't answer, but he gripped his rifle a little more firmly.

The current grew stronger; the boat gathered speed. The rat swam after him, gnashing his teeth in anger. "Stop him! Stop him!" the rat shouted to two pieces of straw and a little twig. "Stop him! He hasn't got a passport, and he won't pay the toll!"

The current ran faster and faster, carrying the boat away from the rat toward the end of the tunnel. The tin soldier could see light ahead.

"Perhaps I will be saved." But at that moment he heard a strange roaring sound which seemed to come closer and closer to his little boat. He could now see that where the tunnel ended, the water tumbled down a great waterfall and emptied into the harbor.

There was no hope of stopping the little paper boat. It pitched and swirled and filled with water. The poor tin soldier stood steady as ever, never flinching. He knew he was doomed. He thought of his brothers again, and of the ballerina, and two lines from a poem ran through his head:

"On, on, brave warrior!
On, where death awaits thee!"

The paper boat gave way and the water swirled over the tin soldier's head. He sank toward the bottom and surely would have drowned had not a hungry fish swooped down and swallowed him up, just like that.

Inside the fish it was even darker than it had been in the sewer. There was barely room enough for the little soldier, but he lay there, without letting go of his rifle, steadfast as ever.

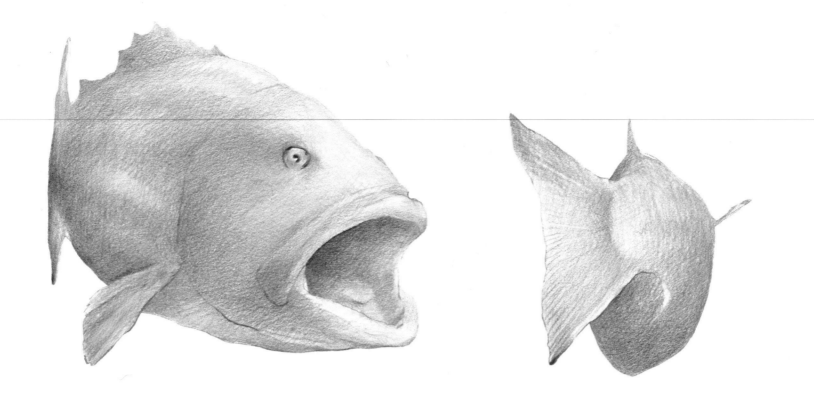

There was no way of knowing when it was day or night, so the tin soldier had no idea how long he lay inside the fish or where the fish was taking him.

All of a sudden the tin soldier felt the fish dart wildly about—up and down, back and forth. "What is happening?" wondered the little soldier. Then it was very still.

A short while later a ray of light came flooding down onto him, and he heard someone exclaim, "Why, here is our little tin soldier!"

The maid picked the soldier up out of the fish and took him to the sink, where she washed him clean and bright as new. Then she carried him into the playroom so that everyone could admire the little traveler who had journeyed inside the belly of a fish.

How strange and wonderful the world is! Here he was, back in the very same room that he had left but a few days before. He was set on the table among the toys he knew. There stood his brothers and the cardboard castle—and most wonderful of all, the little ballerina, as beautiful and as steadfast as ever, in the same blue dress, with the ribbon held by the spangle as bright as a diamond.

The soldier could now see that the ballerina did, in fact, have two legs, that one was extended behind her, nearly hidden by the folds of her skirt. But she was even lovelier than he'd remembered. The little soldier was so happy that he almost shed a tear. But of course that was not proper for a soldier. He looked at her and she at him. He wanted to tell her about his adventures, and of his love for her, which had helped him to be brave when he was afraid. But never a word passed between them.

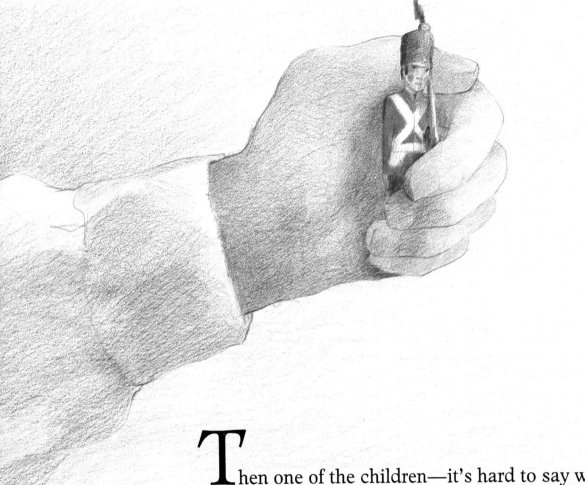

Then one of the children—it's hard to say which one because it all happened so quickly—grabbed the tin soldier, opened the door to the woodstove, and tossed him into the fire. Who knows why. No doubt the troll had a part in it.

The tin soldier stood steadfast while the flames leapt and danced around him. He felt the great heat but wasn't sure if it was from the flames or from the love that burned inside him.

The soldier gripped his rifle and kept his eyes fixed on the ballerina as she stood in front of the castle. He thought that she smiled at him. . . .

A sudden breeze fluttered in through an open window, catching the little paper dancer and lifting her up. Like a tiny fairy she whirled in the air, her spangle glistening as it caught the light—and she flew right into the stove. She flared up for a moment, then she was gone.

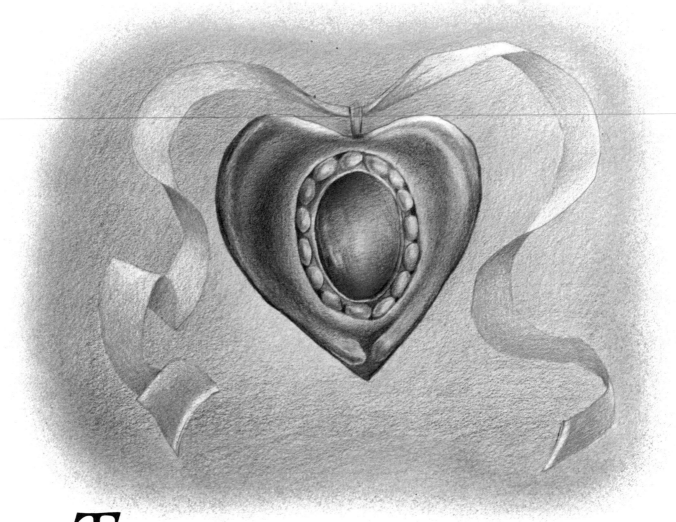

The next day, when the maid was cleaning out the ashes from the stove, a sparkle caught her eye. She pushed aside the ashes with her fingertip and discovered a little tin heart—all that remained of the soldier. She turned the heart over in her hand, and there was the spangle from the ballerina's ribbon. It had melted against the soldier's heart and was now a part of it.

The maid kept the spangled heart. She polished it and made it into a locket to wear around her neck to remind her of the tin soldier and his ballerina.